A Grave Voyage

An In the Cards Story

By E.N. Chanting

Edited by www.abbywoodland.com

Cover by Maria Ann Green

For everyone on a voyage, your journey starts now, today, you've got this. If you need guidance, you'll find it In The Cards!

Blurb

Welcome to In The Cards, a twenty-two author collection of standalone thriller and horror short stories. In this series, you'll find stories inspired by the meaning of a specific Tarot Card, thoughtfully written with that thread woven through. Whether you're a Tarot Card lover or not, you'll find thrillers and horrors that will creep under your skin and into your thoughts. *Knowledge of Tarot Cards is not necessary to read or enjoy these stories.*

Sandra wins a trip on a cruise through the lottery. She's excited and determined to be in control of her future as a new, more adventurous woman. When she meets Jay, a handsome member of the onboard security staff, she thinks she's in for an ocean romance.

Every time they try to spend time together he's called away for another passenger emergency. It seems the people aboard this ship are disappearing and dying at an alarming rate. When the danger becomes too much, Sandra abandons her trip and Jay. But he's not finished with her yet.

Sandra is thrilled to win a cruise and it sets her on the path to becoming the person she wants to be, fun, outgoing, in control. She vows to be different from who she is at home, to grow into a new version of herself. When she meets Jay, a member of onboard security, she takes the opportunity to try out the *New Sandra.* As their relationship blooms she finds herself making positive changes and falling for him. But when he discovers her secret everything begins to fall apart. To hold on to who she is, she needs to choose between fleeing or changes she's not ready to make.

Make sure you come back and check out the other stories, because you never know what's In The Cards.

Baby Moon by Sara Lea

Fallen Angel by Brooke Montoya

Justice by Danielle Fear

The Court of Shadows by Dina Cahaney

Lovers by Tayler Vaughn

The Cure That Kills by Jeremy Fowler

A Hollow Space by Carly Black

A Lethal Tempest by M.A. Green

Light At The End by A.V. Donaldson

A Breathing House by Jed Kent

Stepping into The Star by D.M. Foley

Holy Water by Kathryn Trattner

A King's Ransom by Jeff VanOudenhove

A Grave Voyage by E.N. Chanting

Insomnaria by Sienna Rae

Work in Progress by Erica Damon

Reap What You Sow by M.A. Savino

The Hanged Man by A.C. Hessenauer

The Lion Within by Kay Elem

Play Your Cards Right by Heather S. Chauvin

The End by Cedar Rose

Eight Rooms of Isolation by Nicolasa Desantiago

Content Trigger Warnings

Contains: Murder, death, assault, DV, explicit language, sexual situations

Contents

Represents overcoming challenges and gaining victory through maintaining drive and self-control. It comes to make you stronger as you strive to achieve your goals. You may embrace your path with enthusiasm and harness the momentum for personal growth.

Chapter One

"You're going to be very lucky. A great adventure is in your future." When the tarot card reader said those words, I never believed I'd be here just a few weeks later.

The ship's name, *Majestic Fantasy,* echoed in my head, sounding like an adventure of a whole new kind, wild and free. The closer I got, the bigger the ship appeared towering over me, a mere mortal, on the dock beneath a behemoth of a self-contained magical kingdom. It was exhilarating in a way I'd never felt before. I just knew this was it. I was going to be different on this trip instead of hiding in the shadows like a mouse. I was going to be a beacon of fun in a sparkly dress. Plastering a smile on my face, I greeted every person I passed with a warm "hello," giving them a primo view of my pearly white teeth and deep dimples. My mother always said I had the face to launch a ship in Troy; let's see if that pans out today in Tampa, Florida.

"Good morning, madam, and welcome aboard the *Majestic Fantasy!* Please tell me your name and show me your passport, so I may direct you to your quarters." An overly tanned man announced while looking me over like a piece of meat.

"Good morning, here you go." I held out my passport for him to take and let him discover my name on the document himself.

"Ah, Miss Robertson, I see you're one of our lottery winners. Congratulations! We have a very special cabin for your stay. You'll be on the Elite Deck, the first elevator will take you there. This black card will unlock the elevator and open your Elite Suite. The captain has requested you join him for dinner this evening. All the details of your itinerary will be in the blue folder in your quarters. Please just press the *service* button on your cabin phone if you need anything at all."

He smiled wide with a gleam in his eye that made me uncomfortable while placing the card and a map in my hand, along with my passport. But I'm a whole new person on this ship and I won't let him change my plans. I smile back, ignoring the discomfort it causes in my stomach.

"Thank you. I'm looking forward to all the amenities this ship has to offer."

"Excellent. Have a fantastic time."

My body was carried along by the crowd onto the entry-level of the massive floating adult playground. My eyes travel far and wide observing all the glimmering extravagance that dripped from every surface. It was as if the main entry hall was decorated by the riches hoarded by dragons. From the glamorous chandeliers to the way the gemstone-studded wall coverings sparkled, reflecting the light in prismatic refractions that rivaled a kaleidoscope. It was the most decadent room I had ever been in, and I was mesmerized by the opulence.

People bumped into me if I stopped, even for a moment, to gawk at everything in a room that must be over forty feet high. I didn't want to be in their way, so I found the elevator and unlocked it with my black card, then I used it again to work the elevator sending it up to the top passenger deck. My room was near the end of a long corridor, and had a double door entry, adding to my expectations of grandeur on the other side.

There was no disappointment when I pushed open one of the doors, sunlight beamed across every shiny surface, causing the whole room to glow with an ethereal light. The magic was overwhelming in the best way. How could such a large room be all for me? There was an elegant, and overly indulgent living room, with soft velvet furnishings and glimmering metallic accents. Crystals adorned the chandeliers in the main area and above the massive king-sized bed. The covers looked posh, and there were so many fancy pillows I was almost afraid to touch them. I'd never remember how they were all placed so perfectly.

But the most spectacular feature of this room were the large windows that took up one entire wall the room, it felt like I was floating above the water below. This room is built out past the frame of the base ship and extended far enough that when I looked straight down through the massive panels of glass, all I saw was water. There were other ships in the port, but they seemed miniscule compared to my perch high above them. An air of superiority filled me and I felt just a bit taller. I just knew this was going to be the best adventure of my entire life.

My suitcases have already been brought to my room, and they're placed on stands to aid in unpacking them. Making quick work of it, I placed all my toiletries on the counter, and the edge of the soaking tub. The separate shower had luxury shampoo and body wash, while the tub had a bottle of bubbles that smelled like heaven. I could hardly wait to take a bath. The windows have a screen for privacy, but it rolls out of sight with the press of a button for a view while bathing at sea. The stars on the ocean, without any light pollution, must be stunning. I could soak in the tub while gazing at them. A sigh left me at the thought.

When I finished unpacking, I looked through my closet and admired the fancy dresses I purchased with the cash portion of my prize. It was just ten-thousand dollars, but it was plenty for a woman like me to purchase gowns to wear on a cruise. That was the intention of the prize money, to make the trip a fun experience, not an expense you wouldn't enjoy. Who knew the Florida Lottery Commission was so considerate?

Never having played the lottery, I didn't know they gave out such interesting prizes, but I'm thrilled it turned out this way. My silver dress would be perfect for the first dinner aboard the *Majestic Fantasy,* and with the captain no less.

The ship's massive horn let out one long blast, signaling we were getting underway. Not wanting to miss a moment of this adventure, I grabbed my purse and headed to the nearest railing to wave at strangers as we pulled away from the port. Everyone around me cheered and waved like it was New Year's Eve and the clock just hit midnight. It was a festival on the decks of the ship, and this was only the beginning.

Wanting to explore before lunch, I found my way onto the main deck with all the shops and food. An ice cream shop sat next to a pizza buffet and Starbucks already had a line. It's like being in a mall, at a carnival in Time's Square, or maybe the Vegas strip all at once. Joyful chaos ensues at every turn, and I liked it. The energy and excitement of all the people was contagious, and I felt ready to tackle anything.

When I found the pool area, three different servers tried to give me a drink with an umbrella and a pick stacked with fruit. When the fourth one offered, I gave in. Who could resist such a fun cocktail? It's the ideal drink for a tropical getaway to paradise, fruity punch with a hint of coconut and a strong dose of rum. What more could a girl ask for?

Before I could find a seat with an interesting view to imbibe with my spirits, a man in a uniform approached me with a smile.

"That looks so delicious, are you enjoying the ship so far?" His dark brows raise with the question.

"I'm so amazed by the sheer size of the ship, all the things to do, and places to explore. I got a little overwhelmed and decided to have a break." I reply holding up my drink for emphasis on the *break.*

"Yeah, it can be a bit much, especially on the first day. By tomorrow you'll know all the best places to find fun. I'm Jay, what's your name?"

"Sandra. Do you work on the ship?"

"I'm with the security division on board."

"Oh. Is there much crime on a ship like this?"

His face tensed for a brief moment then his smile returned, "Mostly just someone having too much fun or a misunderstanding. Not much in the line of serious crimes, don't worry. You'll probably never even know if anything like that happens. Don't let it concern you, just enjoy your trip."

"Do they tell you not to discuss the crimes with guests?" I questioned with a smirk.

He looked into my eyes and nodded. "They certainly don't want us scaring the passengers." He smiled and I returned it, a silent communication we both understood he had a job to do, and scaring paying customers wouldn't help him keep it.

"What type of schedule does a person in the security department work on a ship like this?" I asked with a teasing grin remembering I'm a new person on this boat. I'm not myself; I'm *Fun* Sandra Robertson.

"A security person might get off at nine tonight."

"Where might such a person go when they're off the clock?"

"Probably the Flotation Rotation for a drink. He'd also probably enjoy meeting a passenger there, at about nine-fifteen." He returned my grin with a mischievous glint in his eyes.

"A passenger will be in the same bar around the same time, so perhaps their paths will cross." Holding his gaze I tilted my head in a playful move and his smile grew wider.

"Great. Then I hope their paths intersect. I have to get back to work, it's been a pleasure meeting you, Sandra."

"You too, Jay."

Watching his masculine form disappear into the crowd, I couldn't keep the smile from my face. I'm so proud of my transformation. I've been on this giant boat for just a short time and already I've tried a tropical drink and made a date with a stranger, *go me!*

Feeling the rum a little bit now, I spent time watching people from my comfortable chair and it's an interesting mix of young and old, no kids which was a relief. Not that I don't like children, I just didn't think this was the place for them. How could they have any fun while their parents got drunk and gambled?

My own parents never spent any time with me and I think it's why I'm the way I am now. I'm a loner. I hide in the shadows. I don't really have any friends, and all my family is dead. I focus on my work and not much else, it's why I've decided to be someone else on this cruise. Someone exciting and fun. Who knows, maybe it'll be a permanent transformation.

After a walk around more of the ship, I decided it was time to indulge in the fabulous tub in my room. We're away from shore now, so I could open those blinds and watch the sea while I soaked. Then I was putting on that silver dress and turning into a fairy princess at the ball, *well at least at the dinner.*

Chapter Two

As I waited for my planned chance encounter with an incredibly handsome security officer, after a boring dinner with the captain and the other lottery winners, I watched people around me toss back shots, gulp champagne, and act like drunk college students. It was hilarious, and I was glad I decided to limit my own consumption—so far I wasn't embarrassing myself.

My dimples popped as I spotted Jay entering the club. He was taller than I remembered. His dark eyes found me and his bright smile matched mine. Waving to let me know he saw me, he made a stop at the bar for a beer before striding over to my table for two.

"Wow! You're even prettier than I remembered from this morning. You look incredible." He leaned in and gave me a kiss on the cheek. Trying to keep my embarrassment-free streak alive, I hid my wide eyes and opened mouth, surprised by his intimate greeting.

"You look taller than I remembered." My cheeks heated as I kicked myself for being awkward.

He chuckled and leaned close again.

"You should relax, you're on vacation." His eyes searched mine while I tried to think of a witty reply.

"I'm trying." Rolling my eyes at myself, I knew I was blowing this, and I dug deep to find the new Sandra.

"What are your plans for tomorrow?" he asked, throwing me a bone.

"I'm not sure. Some of the onboard activities sound fun. Since it's a day at sea, I thought I might do some shopping."

"Do you gamble?"

"No. I've never tried it. Do you?"

"Once in a while. The trick is to only take as much money as you can afford to lose, then spend the playing time trying to make it last as long as possible, until you inevitably lose it all. Just enjoy the games."

"Like sex." His eyes went wide and he sputtered on his beer as my cheeks heated, but I smirked without further comment.

Now we're talking, New Sandra.

Laughing, he touched my arm and said, "Exactly."

His eyes had a new sparkle in them and I was feeling warm all over now.

Before I could shock him with another overly forward remark, a woman screamed. It was a bloodcurdling sound, and everyone who heard it turned to see what happened. The woman was holding up bloody hands, her hair was a tangled mess, and she had mascara streaked down her face. She ran to the nearest person and grabbed his chest, smearing it with blood while pulling on his lapels.

"He's DEAD! Help me!" she screamed.

"I'll be right back," Jay said as he patted my hand and ran towards the woman.

I watched as he showed the woman his identification, guided her away from the man she covered in blood, and helped her to a chair. She began to cry hysterically and couldn't articulate what had happened as she gasped.

Several people surrounded the woman, and someone handed her a bottle of water while someone else offered a shot glass of something coppery brown. She took the water and tried to get her words out while people fussed around her. The music turned off and the lights came up, the fantasy of an exotic nightclub vanished in an instant. Some of the guests left, while others filmed the action with their cell phones.

Not wanting to be in the way, and having nothing to offer to help with the situation, I quietly left the too bright dance club, and went for a walk along the deck to gaze at the moonlight over the water. My feet took me the entire length of the ship until I ended up at the stern to watch our wake trail behind the giant floating city. It's still amazing to me that a hunk of metal this large can float without toppling over. I understand the physics, it just doesn't make sense to my eyes staring at such a top-heavy vessel.

While I'm admiring the view and enjoying the breeze on my face, I spot a couple having an argument. He's tall and handsome, but obviously over the limit as he stumbles and waves his arms wildly. The woman is also tall with gorgeous red hair, a compliment to the beauty of this couple. They could be models, they look so perfect. But neither one of them is happy, the gorgeous woman swipes tears from her eyes while he tries to plead his case, reasoning away whatever he did wrong.

Stepping a little closer, I can make out their words. He's in trouble for flirting with a waitress at the bar when the woman went to the restroom. He's obviously a dog who thought he could get away with it. He's probably gotten away with it before, when he was sober and not so sloppy. The beautiful woman looks heartbroken, and the next words I catch are from her telling him she can't do this any longer. Because he's not 100%, he does the wrong thing and angrily blames her for his shortcomings.

She shakes her head, her eyes following him as he storms off. Then with a deep breath and more tears, she quietly leaves me as the only person on the back of the ship. With the scene over, my eyes return to the view and I think about how lucky I am not to be tied down to anyone while I have this amazing adventure to enjoy. Tomorrow will be the first full day of trying out the *New Sandra* in a new environment. I plan to seek out fun new experiences and meet some new people. By the time this ship returns to its home port, the *New Sandra* will be the *only* Sandra and I can't wait.

When my eyes open to the warm glow of the rising sun shining across my lovely cabin, I start my day with a smile. Today is going to be an adventure, and I can't wait for some fresh experiences. I hope I cross paths with Jay sooner, rather than later. Our date coming to an abrupt end was highly disappointing. With destiny calling me, I get showered and dressed in record time, ready for a decadent breakfast to begin the day.

The line for the breakfast buffet isn't too long, and I'm quickly seated with a huge plate of mini crepes covered in whipped cream, fruit, and who knows what else. I almost hate to cut into the perfection of it, but my stomach overrides my visual appreciation, in favor of letting my tastebuds enjoy the masterpiece. As I shovel in the last bite, a commotion near the captain's table garners my attention.

The captain isn't in attendance but some other officers are seated with guests. The stunning woman from the deck last night is beginning to get hysterical as she pleads with one of the officers. He's trying to calm her without success, and his table mates step up to help. The woman looks as though she hasn't slept, her skin is pale, her eyes rimmed in red, her mouth tense. I wouldn't have even realized it was the same woman if not for her brilliant fiery hair.

Before I can lean over to hear what's going on, the chair next to me is pulled out, and I look up to see Jay taking a seat.

"Hi. How are you this morning?" I ask.

"I wanted to apologize for last night. I'm sorry I had to jump into work before we could even speak."

"It's okay. Duty calls, right? Did everything turn out all right with that screaming lady?"

His head shakes and he looks pained, "Not really. Her husband was stabbed and we're fairly sure she did it. We have her locked in the brig."

"There's a jail on a cruise ship?" My voice rose to a high pitch with shock.

"Unfortunately, people commit crimes even on cruise ships. We don't usually have a murder suspect in there. The most common infractions are too much alcohol and a little bit of theft. Sometimes we find illegal drugs, and we have a K-9 unit that checks the bags before they go ashore in any port."

"Wow. I had no idea. My home town doesn't have much crime. Where I live, it's practically safe to leave your doors unlocked."

"Never do that!"

"I don't. But I could." I can't help smiling at him. He's so handsome and I'm fascinated by his job.

When I was a kid, a teacher gave me some Nancy Drew Mysteries to read and I always thought it would be fun to solve crimes for a living.

His eyes are on the captain's table where the situation seems to be escalating. The redhead is crying now, and one of the officers is letting her hold onto him, while he looks incredibly uncomfortable trying to console a stranger.

"Do you need to go over there?" I ask.

"Nah, I'm off this morning. She had a fight with her husband last night, and he didn't come back to her cabin. He's probably sleeping it off somewhere, hopefully not in another woman's cabin." He looks at me and smiles. "Let's do something. You already ate breakfast, so let's find something fun to do, then I'll take you to lunch later."

"That sounds perfect."

We leave together, and his hand finds my waist as he guides me from the restaurant and past the disturbance at the captain's table. Happy to be away from the drama, we aim for the gift shops on the shopping deck and spend the next three hours entertaining ourselves with floppy hats, flowered shirts, and memorabilia from the cruise line. We get a foot massage at the spa, smoothies from the poolside bar, and play mini-golf on the upper deck. He's a sweet gentleman who makes my stomach flutter with butterflies, and I haven't laughed this much in a long time. It's the perfect morning, until we enter the restaurant for lunch, and he gets a call requiring him to check in with the security office.

"I'm so sorry. They have an emergency and it's all hands-on-deck."

"Literally," I quip, trying to maintain a bit of the jovial mood from only a moment ago. He smiles, but his jaw is tense.

"I'll make it up to you. Will you have dinner with me?"

"I'd be delighted."

"I'll pick you up from your cabin at seven?"

"Perfect. I'll see you then."

Eating alone is lonely after spending so much time with Jay this morning. It feels cold and dreary without him. Finishing as quickly as possible so I can move out into the sunshine isn't what I had in mind, but it works. Locating a lounge chair on the deck near the pool, I settled in to relax for a bit and do some people watching. Pretending not to notice this is *Old Sandra* behavior, isolating myself and acting like a wallflower, I convince my inner voice to give me a break while I rest up for what I hope will be an exciting night.

After a short nap and two fruity virgin drinks, I aimed for my cabin to take a real nap and then get ready for my date.

Chapter Three

The knock on my cabin door comes at precisely seven o'clock, and I can't help grinning like a teenage girl going on her first date. When I open the door, I'm greeted by a stunningly handsome man whose eyes twinkle with promises of a sinfully good time. I return his smile with a bit of mischief in my own gaze, because if I have anything to do with it, he won't be sleeping in his own quarters tonight.

"Wow! You look incredible."

"Thank you. You're looking quite incredible yourself."

He leads me to the fancy restaurant on board, and we're seated at the chef's table inside the kitchen in a dark corner. It's fascinating watching the culinary staff rush around as they prepare five-star meals of perfection. The wine flows, and the scents of the spices sprinkled in everything are borderline erotic.

"So, tell me more about your life beyond this boat," he requests.

"There's not much to tell. I'm boring, so much so that I promised myself I would try to be more relaxed and go on some adventures while I'm on this trip."

"What sort of adventure are you looking for?" His fingertips travel up my arm to my shoulder in a sensual touch that lights up my insides.

His gentle caress brings a grin to my lips. "I don't know. What type of adventure would you suggest?"

He grips my upper arm, pulling me close, his lips brushing mine. His eyes search my own, perhaps for permission. But the *New Sandra* doesn't hesitate and meets his mouth in a soft connection. My lashes touch my cheeks and my tongue pries between his pillowy lips, deepening our kiss. His tongue touches mine and swirls as they intertwine, we explore each other, drawing a gentle moan from my throat.

Then I remember we're in a galley filled with people, and end it with a promise to continue when we're in private. His knowing smirk makes my insides heat up further. We finish our meal and indulge in dessert, a decadent chocolate confection that tantalizes the tastebuds.

"Tell me about your day. You had that emergency earlier, so you probably had some excitement while I napped."

"I suppose you could say that. There's a missing passenger. After a fruitless search, they declared him as lost overboard."

"Oh my God. He killed himself?"

"Maybe. Or maybe someone pushed him. We're investigating both possibilities, but don't worry, I'll keep you safe."

"Thank you. I've never had a protector before."

"Why is that?"

"My family, they weren't the best caregivers. I learned to take care of myself at an early age."

"Well, I'm here now and I'll do everything in my power to safeguard you."

"I appreciate it." He takes my hand and leads me to a quiet spot on the deck. The moon is hanging above the horizon and reflecting on the water. As we walk along, he continues to hold my hand.

When I open my eyes it's morning and I feel excited about the day's adventures. Today I'm visiting the shores of Cozumel. I signed up for a jeep tour to San Gervasio to see the ancient temples, plazas, and pyramids. The brochures say they think the site was built to worship the goddess Ixchel, the Mayan goddess of fertility. Not anything I'm looking for at the moment, but I suppose a blessing for the future wouldn't be unwanted.

I won't see Jay until I return to the ship tonight. He asked me to join him for dinner once again. Thinking of him makes my insides warm. He's so tall and handsome, I feel like a beautiful princess in his arms, not the lonely *Sandra* who existed before this trip. They say if you make a change and keep at it for two weeks, it will become a part of your routine. This cruise only lasts for one, so the most difficult part of my transformation will happen once I'm back home. That's the real challenge. It's easy to be someone else where everything is new and exciting, and where nobody knows you are truly a lame loser. But I'm determined to make this change stick. I must. I can't live another day as the old, boring, *Sandra.*

The small group of tourists joining me for this trek are friendly, and we chat about what we've learned about the ruins. Two young couples are excited to gain the fertility blessings, and three older couples are just interested in the historical significance of the site. The other single guests are four women and two men, none of whom pique my interest.

But since I'm the *New Sandra,* I speak with them all, joking and laughing as the tour company works on dividing us into each vehicle. I end up in the bright green one with an older couple and one of the single women. They're pleasant enough, but I'm pleased when the ancient ruins poke above the trees. When we wind around on the dirt track, the forest parts and the stone structures magically appear. I instantly feel small and insignificant.

It's overwhelming to be in the presence of something so old, and to contemplate the changes in the world during the time these structures have stood here. From ancient worship to tourist attraction, the simple people who built them never imagined how long they would stand guard over an ever growing and changing society.

The next three hours are spent investigating each building, reading all the information, and taking pictures. Our group fans out and agrees to meet our drivers when we're finished. I wander around each structure, at the edge of the tall forest. It's a little cooler and there are interesting sounds of local fauna...monkeys, parrots, maybe even a jaguar. Hopefully, there aren't any snakes nearby, they have some deadly ones in this part of the world.

Deciding to venture just a bit more into the wilderness, I keep sight of the ruins while I observe the interesting plants and insects that move around without notice. It's a well populated slice of all things mystical forest, and I rejoice in the small creatures who catch my eye. Following a bright flutter of blue wings, I step a little further into the shade of the tall and luscious trees.

A man I don't recognize from our group walks into the woods about twenty feet from me. His vision is sharply focused on something I can't see, and I doubt he noticed me. I watch him disappear into the shadows and it makes me curious. Who is he? What's he doing? I follow after him and promise myself I won't go too far into the trees. I catch sight of his blue shirt and walk carefully to keep quiet. I follow him deeper into the darker corners of the forest.

When two men appear and greet him with a handshake, I hide behind a tree and use my phone to video record what they're doing. I have the distinct feeling this is some sort of illegal exchange, and my inner sleuth is chomping at the bit to capture a bad guy and unravel a mystery. I can't hear what they're saying, their voices are soft and they're too far away. But their boisterous laughter reaches me easily, and it sounds sinister over the sounds of nature in this peaceful setting. After a few more minutes of talking, they separate and the man in the blue shirt turns back towards the ruins, of course I follow him.

When I exit the barely-there-path, the man in the blue shirt is no longer visible. I straighten my clothes and redo my loose ponytail before joining some people from my group. We all smile at each other, but we're less talkative than when we arrived, tired from the hours spent exploring the ancient history of the Mayans.

Back on board the *Majestic Fantasy,* my first priority is a shower to wash away the jungle sweat and who knows what else. Getting dressed in another new dress, I ponder where my security officer will take me for dinner. We're still in port with a sailing time of midnight, plenty of time to go ashore and experience the local cuisine. Excitement blooms in my stomach, as my tall, dark, and handsome date fills my mind with images of kissing him, and maybe more.

The knock on my door is right on time once again. My gorgeous security officer smiles when he sees me. My own face hurts, I'm smiling so hard.

"Every time I see you, I think, *wow-she's even prettier than the last time I saw her.*"

"You sure know how to make a girl feel confident. Where are we going?"

He held my hand and guided me to the elevator, "We're going to this little place with amazing food. They catch the fish every day and the chef is world class."

"It sounds great. How was your day?"

"It was good, but another passenger went missing. Don't tell anyone. I'm not supposed to share that information." He smiles and winks, causing my knees to wobble.

It's hard not to grab hold of him and kiss him silly. Even though the *New Sandra* may be fun, she's not aggressive. I should probably work on being a little more forward, and asking for what I want.

When we get into the taxi, he helps me with a hand on my waist. The warmth of his touch sends tingles through me, raising goosebumps on my skin. We huddle close, and his fingers make little circles on my arm as the driver tells us some of the history of this part of the city. The restaurant is in a small building that looks like a house. I'm not expecting much, but I'm pleasantly surprised by the ambiance of the candles and crystal chandeliers in the cozy space. It's more upscale than it appears from outside. Our table is in a quiet corner, the food is delicious, and the company is perfect.

"Have you found that other missing passenger yet?"

"No. He's officially lost overboard, his fiance` left to go home. Now, today, we're missing another passenger who never returned from an excursion."

"Oh, wow. Does that happen often?"

"More than you would think. Usually, it's something dumb and they just missed their return transportation. We'll probably find him on board later, and he'll have a story about his wild adventures on vacation. Although, one time a missing passenger had a heart attack and it took us three days to find him in a hospital."

"That's awful. Is it usually single travelers who go missing?"

"No. We've had entire families miss the boat. They end up spending a fortune to get a flight home, though sometimes they fly to the next port to catch the ship and finish their vacation. It's just one of the many fun things I get to do at my job."

"You don't seem all that thrilled with your job. Why do you do it?"

"When I got divorced, I had been working at the Tampa Police Department for eight years, but I needed to get away. A fresh start, new scenery. When I heard the cruise line was hiring, I decided to give it a try for a while. But I miss being a detective on land. This job is less detective and more babysitter. I'm over it."

"I understand that. My job gets old every spring, summer can't come fast enough. But then the new year begins in the fall and I'm re-energized and ready to mold young minds once again."

"You don't look like any teacher from my school days, you're much too pretty. When I was in school, I would've flunked out if you were my teacher. I would've spent all my time fantasizing about you instead of learning. Thankfully all my teachers were old and frumpy, so I was able to graduate." His charming smile makes my stomach flutter.

His hand is warm in mine, and he leans in and brushes his lips against my own. The thrill of sensation it sends through my veins collects in my core, and I deepen our kiss. He's as excited as I am, and he quickly pays our check so we can find privacy. We urge our driver to hurry, getting us back to the ship in record time. Our steps are hurried as we rush to my room, unable to keep our hands off each other any longer.

We almost fall into my elite room when the door opens, and our clothes leave a trail to the bedroom. Our kisses are frantic, our hands roaming each other's bodies seeking the places with the most response. His hands are large, warm, and calloused. They excite me as he caresses every inch of my skin, as if he's worshiping a goddess. Feeling hot and turned on, we climbed onto my large bed. The cool sheets ease some of my overheated condition, but his kisses focus the heat on the places his lips meet, and he makes certain to cover all my most sensitive skin.

His chest is a sculpted work of art with tattoos that enhance the view. A grim reaper dominates the scene and it speaks to me on a primal level. When he enters me, it's as if he was meant to be close to me all along, our bodies as one. We move together seeking the same release, clinging to one another as we reach the simultaneous climax of our efforts. Falling back on to the bed, we both gasp for air as the remaining jolts of pleasure work through us. I'm filled with a surge of joy, and it breaks free in a silly giggle.

He turns onto his side, his hand on my hip.

"What's so funny?" He's unable to fight the grin on his own lips.

"Just...happy."

"Good. I really like you, Sandra."

"I like you too."

"Do you think you'd be willing to go on a date after we get back?"

"I think I'd like that."

I snuggled into his chest and he wrapped his arms around me.

Chapter Four

When my eyes adjusted to the morning light coming through the wall of windows, I immediately missed the warmth from the arms I fell asleep cuddled within. His side of the bed is cold. Dragging myself up from the soft mattress, I spotted a note propped against the lamp on my nightstand.

Sandra, It was so difficult to leave you, but I had to go to work. Please have dinner with me tonight. I'll get you at 7pm. -J

There was a knock at my door. I threw on my robe and answered.

A woman with a cart filled with cloche covered dishes asked to enter. She left with a smile after I signed the receipt. I started lifting the lids and found pancakes, bacon, fruit, eggs, and a small bouquet of pink roses. It was sweet and delicious. I knew without a doubt Jay had sent this breakfast for me. He's so considerate, I could see us having many breakfasts in bed in the future.

With a song in my heart and a permanent smile on my lips, I faced my day. The ship sailed all night, and we were docking at our next port when I went out on the balcony. I watched the precision of the team on the dock as they brought the *Majestic Fantasy* into her berth.

When I went to the large entry lobby, there were cruise personnel helping passengers find their way to various excursions. I decided to join a party going on a shopping trip in town. It was another beautiful day in paradise, and I worked on spending more of my lottery winnings.

The town was quaint and old fashioned in the best way, almost like the Florida Keys. I could imagine a pirate ship pulling into port and Jack Sparrow drinking his way through the women and rum. He's the image of every imaginary pirate once you've seen the movie too many times. The kids in my class love him, and when we play dress up at least one child is the captain we all love.

I bought some souvenirs for some of my co-workers and for my classroom. The pirate items will go right into my dress-up trunk, and the shark teeth will go into the animal bin. We had a Florida animal expert visit last year who brought snakes, a possum, and an alligator. The kids went nuts over the skins, bones, and teeth she brought. The principal purchased a kit with various bones and teeth for the media center, but I was building my own for my classroom.

When I went back to the ship, there were some kids diving into the water to retrieve coins the tourists threw in. They were impressive swimmers, but it broke my heart seeing them working at such a young age. But poverty doesn't discriminate. Any age, sex, or race, can struggle with it. Once I was back in my room and had my purchases safely packed away, I relaxed on the balcony for a while.

My whole life has changed because of this trip. The *New Sandra,* had done things the old me never would've. She wouldn't have even come on this trip in the first place, let alone ventured into port or slept with a man she just met. I liked the new me, and I wasn't going back to the old me ever again. I would enjoy this new me to the fullest, taking what I want, doing what I want, and being who I want. My smile felt a little devilish, but the new me might just be a little bit evil, and I'm okay with it.

When Jay arrived, I was ready and waiting for him. The ship was setting sail again at eight o'clock, so we're dining onboard. But instead of one of the fancy restaurants, Jay took me to a little buffet place mixed into some of the shops on the upper deck. I hadn't noticed it before, and he raved about the food and quiet atmosphere.

We were seated in front of a window, and with the dark tint, we were able to watch the sunset without being blinded. It was stunning. We were silent as we watched the largest star in our world dip below the sea. There's always a flash when the sun disappears, and it's technically known as *Green Flash.* It's an optical phenomenon that only lasts seconds, but it makes me feel special, like I got to see behind the curtain for just a moment.

Jay and I laugh and chat all evening, and I like him even more with every moment we spend together. He's smart and kind, his heart is in the right place, and he's very considerate of me. He always checks in before making a decision, and he asks if I need anything. I've never dated anyone like him before, and I hope this relationship will continue to grow once we leave the ship.

"I decided to put in my notice to leave the ship's security team. I have some money saved up, and I can take my time finding a new department. There's so many local municipalities, I can join a force with a smaller crew and be the lead detective."

"That's exciting. You'd be great as the boss."

"More likely I'd be the only detective in a small department, but I'm okay with that. You wouldn't mind if I had to leave on a call during the night would you?"

My stomach filled with the flutter of butterfly wings hearing him plan for *our* future.

"No. I wouldn't mind." He looked into my eyes with approval, giving me another boost to my confidence.

"I'm glad. Want to go for a walk in the moonlight?"

"Yes."

We held hands and talked about our plans for after the cruise. The places he's going to apply, the plans he has to purchase a house, and move out of his studio *divorce* apartment. I spoke about my ideas to expand some of the programs in my class. Reading is so important to me, and I want the kids to love it all their lives like I do.

When we got to the bow of the ship, the wind was blowing, and my hair was torn loose from its updo. He sheltered me in a cove, and then he leaned in for a romantic, moonlit kiss that curled my toes. His tall frame is solid with muscle, and my own is more solid than I look. My pale skin and lack of bulk leaves people to come to the conclusion I'm not anyone to fear. But people always underestimate women.

Hidden in the shadows, we went unnoticed by a couple who were arguing nearby. It interrupted our delicious kiss, and disrupted the flow of where our romance was heading. Annoyed, I was ready to sneak off for some quiet privacy, but Jay had another plan.

He held out his badge, "Hello folks. Is there anything I can help you with?"

The man startled and grabbed the woman's arm, pulling her behind him with unnecessary force. She grimaced and anger clenched my hands into fists.

"No! I don't need shit from you. Why don't you go find a tourist eating too much at the buffet to harass?"

"I just wanted to make sure everything is all right. You seemed upset. Is there anything I can help with?" Jay replied in a neutral tone.

"We don't need shit from you. Come on, Lisa, let's go, now!" He dragged her off and I felt upset on her behalf. The poor woman was obviously frightened by the man pulling her around. I have no doubt he's her husband, as they wore matching wedding bands. I want to help her escape his clutches, but there's nothing Jay or I can do.

"Let's follow them at a distance. I just want to make sure the woman is safe."

"Sure. I'm always up for a spy mission," I agree.

"Were you a detective in another life?"

"I think I was. Maybe Nancy Drew?"

"Wasn't she a fictional character?"

Our friendly banter continued as we followed the couple, we pretended we weren't following them. We were just walking and chatting without any interest in them. When they entered their cabin we hid around the corner, then Jay listened at their door for any commotion.

"I think they're going to sleep, he seemed to calm down. There wasn't any more yelling."

"Thank goodness. Want to check my cabin for anything amiss?" I said with a wink, and what I hoped qualified as a sultry smile.

"You know it, gorgeous."

He tickled me, and I squealed then jogged away as fast as possible in my heels. We played our game of chase until we reached the elevator, where I inserted my special black card and we were lifted to my floor. Before we stepped off the gold car, we were already embraced in a passionate kiss. He lifted me by my behind and my legs wrapped around him. Thankfully, my skirt allowed the action without flashing anyone. Not that other passengers were around.

We spent another night wrapped up intimately in each other and when we fell asleep, there were satisfied smiles on our faces.

This time I was up before him, and it was still dark. I went for a run, then grabbed some bagels and coffee at one of the many java stations around the various decks. When I entered my room Jay was dressed and putting on his shoes.

"Hey, I was wondering where you went."

"Just out to grab us some breakfast. Do you have work today?"

"I do. But I go in a little later, and I have to work until ten tonight."

"I guess I'll be dining alone." I frowned.

"Or you could have a late lunch and a snack and dine with me when I'm finished?"

"I could do that." We were on our way back to Florida, stopping one last time in Key West. We sailed all night and would reach the port late this morning.

Jay was finishing his second bagel when his phone rang. It was still early and hours from the start of his shift.

"Yeah? Where? I'm on my way." He hung up and looked at me disappointed.

"What's up?"

"Unfortunately, I have to go. They found a body in a storage area and they need my help."

"Oh no. I'm sorry. I'll have my phone with me, if you have any time, call me and maybe we can meet for lunch or something."

"Maybe. I was hoping to spend more time with you this morning, I'll call you later."

"Okay. Good luck." He kissed me firmly on the lips, and I had the urge to grab hold of him and not let him go, but I didn't. The poor guy has to do his job, at least for a few more weeks.

I spent the day wandering the various decks, shops, and pools. I even tried what Jay suggested at the casino. I only brought twenty dollars with me and played it until it was gone. It only took about forty minutes, but I decided it was worth the entertainment. A dancer from their main stage got into a fight with a bartender, and it was quite the show. Apparently, he slept with a waitress behind her back. Then the *waitress* got in the middle of it, and there were hair extensions and fingernails flying everywhere. It was our own little shipboard, drama-filled soap opera.

The only good thing about it was Jay showed up with two other officers to break up the fight. He saw me, and we were able to sneak off and grab a fast lunch on his break. We got sandwiches and sat outside in the shade.

"The guy's body was mangled in some machinery. We don't know if he did it to himself or if it was foul play. We have all the evidence collected, and when we get back to Tampa, the forensics team will investigate what happened."

"That sounds awful. How do you eat after something like that?"

"On the police force, I learned to eat when I could whether I just saw a gruesome death or not. You have to figure out how to deal with it, or get a different job."

"I remember a student vomited in the cafeteria and that caused three more kids to vomit. Nobody could eat in there for days."

He chuckled.

"I don't think teachers need the iron stomach of a cop."

"You'd be surprised," I smirked.

We said our goodbyes with a kiss and a promise to meet later. I hoped no more people would disappear or end up dead and make him miss our late meal. I love spending time with him. My day continued uneventfully, and when it was finally time to eat with Jay, we agreed to meet at the bar and grill on the *Aloha Deck*.

The food was fast and we were both starving, not having eaten since our lunch at three o'clock. We shared our meals. He had the grouper and I had the crab. It didn't last long, but we slowed down for dessert.

"Are you sure you can help me with this? It's huge!"

"That's what she said."

"Oh, you are a naughty teacher aren't you?" I giggled when he squeezed my bare knee. My dress was more of a club style, and the hem fell above my knees, leaving them exposed to his warm, rough fingers.

"Maybe. So, tell me about that guy's body. Did anyone come up with any more details?"

"We identified him, remember the couple from last night that was arguing?"

"Yeah."

"It was that guy. The wife is a suspect, she's not locked up, but she's not free to leave the ship. When we get to port in Key West, they'll take her in and question her."

"Do you think she did it?"

"No, but there's some evidence it may have been a woman, the drag marks are suspicious. If it wasn't a woman, it was a small guy. We'll figure it out, but most likely it was her. Who else would have a motive? You saw him last night...he was a jerk to her."

"He was. Hopefully, she'll be cleared and live in peace now. Let's hope he has a big life insurance policy."

"Don't worry until there's an ice cream party."

"Why?"

"There's only so much cold storage on board, if we run out of room for bodies we need to clear freezer space."

"You're so bad." We both laughed at his assessment.

We weren't in the mood for a stroll, so we danced in the club for an hour. Once we were tired of that, we went back to my room. I hadn't allowed the stewards to clean my room. I was worried they'd accidentally damage my souvenirs. It was silly, but I wanted to be there if anyone cleaned the room, and I didn't want to wait for them today.

We made short work of our clothes and had a workout on my bed. He was all about pleasing me with his tongue, and I returned the favor. When we were finished, panting, covered in sweat, and enjoying the bliss we found together, we decided to try out my large shower. I had seen some of the coffins they described as a shower in most of the rooms online, so I was very pleased with my jumbo-sized shower. It was big enough for two. Even if one of the two was a big guy.

When we got out of the shower, the bathmat was soaked. Our amorous showering had splashed beyond the confines of the tiled walls. Jay found some more towels to dry the floor and our bodies. When I pulled out an extra towel for my hair, a smaller one fell out of the cubby with it. Before I noticed what happened, Jay was holding up a red stained hand towel with a look of confusion.

"What's this?"

"Ew! Where did that come from?"

"It fell when you grabbed your towel. It looks like blood."

"It does. Why was it in my bathroom?"

"That's a good question. Let's get dressed. I'll call my office and we can get someone up here to figure it out."

With a nod, I quickly dried off and got dressed. As soon as Jay was dressed he found his phone and began to dial. I hit him over the head with the vase of beautiful lilies from the coffee table. He fell to the floor unconscious. Damn, I was hoping to keep him.

Chapter Five

I quickly tied him up with the rope from my bag, just his hands behind his back and a gag over his mouth. The gag was improvised with a scarf. It wasn't long before his eyes blinked a few times and he groaned, most likely coming-to with a headache after that blow to his temple.

"What happened?" he mumbled through the fabric in his mouth.

"You were going to call your security office and I can't allow that. I'm sorry Jay, I really like you."

"Please. Let me talk to you," he forced out through the royal blue silk.

"Only if you promise not to yell." He nodded emphatically. I helped him sit up.

I removed the gag, and he moved his lips, licked them for moisture, then I held a glass of water to them to help his dry mouth. I really do care.

"Please tell me why you're doing this. I really like you. I think I'm falling for you. I don't understand what's happening."

"I like you too, but I can't let you turn me in, I would lose everything."

"Turn you in for what? Please tell me what's going on."

"What do you think is happening? What is your brain telling you that you don't want to believe?"

"You knocked me out after I found a bloody towel. I don't know why you did that."

"You're just trying to manipulate me now. Of course you have some ideas about why I would do that. You just think if you act clueless you can trick me into letting you go. You're a detective for heaven's sake. You can't convince me you're unable to connect the dots."

"If I was to offer a guess, I would think the blood might be from the guy we found mangled. But why would you have it? Why would you kill him?"

"Some people call me a vigilante, others just call me *The Judge.*"

"The serial killer?" All of the color drained from Jay's face. Now he was getting it. He was in serious trouble here and I wasn't anyone to be fooled.

"I see those wheels turning."

"I worked on the case, we all did. We have a profile, a man, middle aged, employed, with a family, living a double life."

"You were wrong. I've never been married, you know I'm not even close to being a man, but I'm employed so you got one point."

"Why?"

"Why do I do it?"

"Yeah. Why do you kill?"

"I grew up in an abusive home. My best friend was raped and beaten by my father in my room. I killed him. She never told anyone what I did. We both lived a much better life after he died. Then I was in college with a girl who was dating an abusive piece of shit. She was smart, really smart, pretty, getting a master's degree, she had everything going for her until she met him. He isolated her from her friends and family, he controlled her and her money. She started flunking classes, and he just tightened his hold on her. When she came to class with sunglasses and makeup hiding the bruises, I knew what was happening. I caught him alone and strangled him in his truck. I waited in the back seat for him. It took all my strength, and I even used my body weight to pull that strap tight. He struggled at first, but then he lost consciousness, and I held his airway closed until his heart stopped. She left school, but she went back and completed medical school. She's a neurosurgeon now, she saves lives every day. He was going to kill her eventually, but I helped her escape."

"That guy from last night, he was abusing his wife, so you killed him?"

"Yeah. It's what I do."

"I...I don't even know what to say."

"I understand. But I can't let you turn me in, too many people need me."

"You're going to kill me?" His eyes were wide.

"I don't want to do that. I like you and you're a good guy, and you don't meet my criteria."

"What are you going to do then?"

"I'm not sure yet." We sat in silence, each of us contemplating where we go from here.

He was probably trying to figure out how to escape, while I figured out how to let him live. When I got tired of sitting, I walked around the room, thinking over my options. If I could find a way to escape while he stayed on the ship without reporting me, that would be ideal. I took a bathroom break and he promised not to move. But

I tied his ankles and put the gag back on for safety's sake. He didn't fight me, but his eyes were sad.

When I returned, I released his mouth and offered him a drink of water and I had a soda. We stared at each other for a long time without speaking. Just drinking our water and soda and watching each other. His was on the coffee table with a straw so he could drink it without hands. I felt bad each time he leaned over for a sip.

"I don't know if I can live with myself if I don't turn you in. I don't want to lie to save myself, even if it's a stupid thing to do. I really like you, my feelings haven't gone away because of this."

"My feelings for you are strong too and I don't want to hurt you. Do you think you can let me go? Let me have a head start?"

"I don't know." His chin hit his chest and I wasn't sure if he was sad or what. Then he snorted before settling into soft snores.

I wiped every surface clean, grabbed my bag, souvenirs, ropes, and all. I untied him and left my cabin. I didn't encounter anyone in the hallway. I made it to the lobby without seeing anyone else. But in the fancy lobby near the exit was the tan man I met when I came on board.

"Miss Robertson! What a pleasure to see you again. I trust you've been having a lovely vacation."

"I have. Thank you so much."

"You're not leaving us here are you? We're having a surprise ice cream party tonight." He eyed my luggage while I grimaced.

"Oh no. I just want to send off some of my souvenirs, so I don't have to lug them onto a plane. Plus, I plan to do some serious shopping in town. I'll need something in which to drag all my new items back here."

With a chuckle and a bright smile he nodded, "Have a wonderful day in port."

"Thank you!"

With that goodbye, I left the boat at the dock and found a taxi. At the airport, I took a flight to Miami. As much as I would have enjoyed staying there for a few days to see the sights, I needed to get home before the ship made it back to Tampa. I took a train from Miami to West Palm Beach, then a bus to Orlando. I rented a car and drove the rest of the way back home. I live in a sleepy little town about forty minutes outside Tampa, along the coast. When I got home, I took anything related to my trip out back and burned it in my firepit.

I had claimed my winnings with a fake ID and went on the ship with my fake name. I wasn't really *Old or New Sandra Robertson.* My fake identification and passport went into the fire along with all my clothes, everything that could have been seen on board was burned to ash.

I returned to my regular life, as *The Judge,* a teacher by day and a vigilante by night. I hoped Jay was all right and returned to Tampa without any lasting effects from my sleeping pills. I didn't read about him as a tragedy from the 'boat murders.' A reporter had picked up on the story after the ship returned to port. It was the highest amount of casualties reported on a ship that hadn't gone down. I was a little proud that I managed to eliminate so many abusers in one vacation. It usually took more time and logistics to plan out one of my murders. This was a sea of opportunities, *pun intended,* and I cashed in.

Epilogue

A knock at the door startled me, but I took a breath settling my nerves, and peered out the window. An unmarked police car stood in my driveway. A man with a gun strapped to his side was at my door, but I couldn't see his face. I slapped on my most innocent smile and pulled open the door.

"Hello, Miss Graves." His dark hair shone in the sunlight, his brown eyes sparkled with delight, his smile was huge, he looked elated.

"Jay? How did you find me?"

"Are you going to ask me in?"

"Are you here to arrest me?"

"Not today."

"Okay." I stepped aside and let him in. What choice did I have, really? "Can I get you something to drink?"

He laughed, "I don't think so, I don't need a nap."

"I'm sorry about that."

"Yeah, you mentioned that in your letter."

"I meant it. Please, have a seat. Are you wearing a recording device?"

He lifted his shirt and emptied his pockets. He didn't even have his cell phone.

"I'm not wired, I'm not here on official business. I just wanted to see you and talk."

"Okay. I'm listening."

"After I got back, I left my job with the cruise line. I got hired on with Mystic Cross Police, I've been looking for you since I got home."

"Why?"

"I missed you. If I'm honest, I was mad you bested me. I wanted to see you again. I wanted to identify *The Judge*...there's a hundred reasons."

"You found me, now what?"

"I'm not sure. In your note you apologized and told me you cared for me. You said you wished there was a way for us to be together. Was that true?"

"It was. The only lies I ever told you were my name and I lied by omission about the guys I killed."

"That's what I thought. I can't stop thinking about you...I almost called you *Sandra.*"

"I'm Kelli."

"I know, it just feels strange to change your name in my head."

"You're still Jay?" He looked into my eyes with hope, it made warmth travel through my body.

"Yep. Would you go to dinner with me? Maybe we can figure out a way to work this out. I can't forget you and I don't want to."

"I've missed you too. But how can we make this work? A cop dating a serial killer seems like a difficult hurdle."

"I don't know. Maybe you can stop killing people, and we can just forget the past?"

"Maybe. Or maybe you could help me remove the scum of the earth?"

"Let's take this one step at a time."

The *New Sandra* turned out to be the *New Kelli.* I quit killing people, we moved in together, and Jay forgot about the past like he promised. We eventually got married and committed ourselves to each other for better or worse, no matter what.

That is until we got new neighbors...when I met the wife she was doing everything she could to cover the fingerprint shaped bruises on her wrist and neck. When I told Jay about it, he looked at me expectantly, waiting for *The Judge* to determine our next step. But whatever I decide, I know he's on board.

The End

Other In The Cards Stories

Baby Moon by Sara Lea

Fallen Angel by Brooke Montoya

Justice by Danielle Fear

The Court of Shadows by Dina Cahaney

Lovers by Tayler Vaughn

The Cure That Kills by Jeremy Fowler

A Hollow Space by Carly Black

A Lethal Tempest by M.A. Green

Light At The End by A.V. Donaldson

A Breathing House by Jed Kent

Stepping into The Star by D.M. Foley

Holy Water by Kathryn Trattner

A King's Ransom by Jeff VanOudenhove

A Grave Voyage by E.N. Chanting

Insomnaria by Sienna Rae

Work in Progress by Erica Damon

Reap What You Sow by M.A. Savino

The Hanged Man by A.C. Hessenauer

The Lion Within by Kay Elem

Play Your Cards Right by Heather S. Chauvin

The End by Cedar Rose

Eight Rooms of Isolation by Nicolasa Desantiago

Acknowledgements

I would like to thank the organizers of this project, Sara Lea (Thornhill), Maria Ann Green, and Erica Damon. They worked long and hard to pull this off. They've also been so kind and patient with those of us who are somewhat clueless. Thank you so very much!

Also, my thanks to the other authors who participated. You're all superstars! It's been such a pleasure working with each and every one of you.

To my ARC readers, and those readers who come after...this means you, writing is a pleasure, but it wouldn't be nearly as rewarding without you. Thank you! Thanks for reading, thanks for reviewing, just—THANK YOU!

About the Author

A writer of romantic suspense and horror who occasionally dips a toe into the paranormal with ghosts, witches, and shifters. She lives on the Florida coast in a haunted house, with her high school sweetheart and 3 goofy Australian Shepherds. E.N. writes most days and can usually be found clicking away on her laptop, with a dog at her feet, and heavy metal music blaring in the background. Ms. Chanting worked as a children's librarian which only enhanced her affection for the written word. She loves to read, spend time with family, and enjoys nature in all forms.

Also by E.N. Chanting

Forces of Nature Series (interconnected world of stand-alones)

Force of Corruption

Force Majeure

Force of Attraction

Force of Addiction-Coming eventually

Violet's Tales

Origin of Violet

Violent

Vile

Violent Night-Coming soon

Stand Alones

Haunted Hunting Camp

The Devil's Affair

Deadly-Go-Round

The Profit-Coming soon

Beautiful Badass-Coming soon

Anthologies

Monsters, Masks, and Mayhem

Pawsitive Beginnings

Pretty Little Slashers II

In the Cards

Silent Saviors

Ink For Blood-Coming soon

Silent Scars-Coming soon

Winter Desires-Coming soon

Join the newsletter on https://www.enchantingauthor.com for a free copy of Origin of Violet

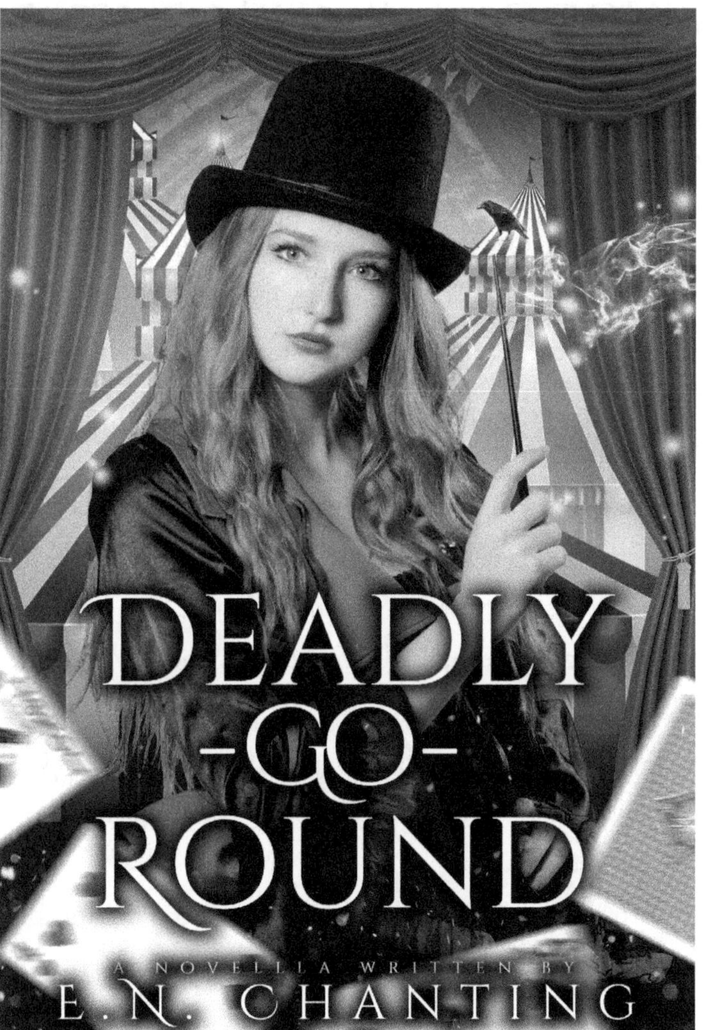
DEADLY
-GO-
ROUND
A NOVELLA WRITTEN BY
E.N. CHANTING

Deadly-Go-Round

CHAPTER ONE

Headstrong and pouting with her headphones on, in the back seat, Rave stubbornly ignores her family's attempts to engage her. Eventually her eyes fall closed, and she blocks them out completely by falling asleep. The SUV speeds along a highway somewhere in the South, the navigation system keeps Read, the patriarch of the family, apprised of his next turn. Random, who just turned eleven, sits next to his sleeping older sister oblivious to her strife, playing his handheld game.

When Rail spots a sign for a park, she asks Read to stop so they can stretch their legs and enjoy the picnic luncheon she packed.

"And we need to walk Rogue, he's been a good boy back there but I'm sure he could use a potty break," Rail explains to Read who's used to her long-winded commentary filled with passive aggressive orders, making this exchange relatively painless.

"Are we stopping?" Random asks excitedly.

"Yes, please wake Rave so she can gather her things."

When the vehicle comes to a stop the doors open, and everyone exits with their arms full. After carrying a load of items to a picnic shelter Read collects Rogue and hooks his leash onto the harness wrapped around the friendly beast. The fluffy black K-9 is a mixed breed of sorts found at the pound. He was on his last day when the Ripley family showed up and got him pardoned from the gallows. He's very attuned to the family and he tries to anticipate their needs. As the newest member of the clan, he does a pretty good job and gets it right most of the time. The rest of the time ends with him under foot and dodging being stepped on.

The dark-haired, sullen, teen-angst-filled Rave rests her forearms on the picnic table and her chin on her hands. Unwilling or uncaring to help, she glowers while Rail hands out the carefully packaged sandwiches and little bags of chips. When a kid's juice pouch is placed in front of her, Rave has had enough. She clicks her tongue, rolls her eyes, and stomps off on her own sans sandwich. She doesn't hear her father calling after her because she dialed up the volume on her music to match her exasperation.

"Just leave her be, she's going to be sorry later when she's hungry and we don't have time to stop for her. How's your sammi, Randy?"

"It has mayo, so it's gross but I'm hungry." He takes another bite and flips his dark curls from his eyes. Rogue is happily panting beneath the table hoping for someone to be clumsy and drop some crumbs his way. He's betting on the boy, if the past holds true, since he's the most likely to share whether it's on purpose or not.

"It shouldn't be too much further to the bed and breakfast, the navigation is acting a little dodgy, but I don't think it's far off this road once we get into Hangman's Bluff. We probably have less than two hours to go," Read says to no one in particular.

"I still don't understand why you wanted to visit this dreary place. Who gives their town such an awful name? It sounds dreadful from just the name alone, though I can't wait to visit the gardens in the town square. You aren't expecting me to go to the museum, are you?" Rail asks her husband who cringes at her accusing tone.

"No. Rave and Randy can join me, or you, whichever they prefer. You can visit the greenhouse and flowers to your heart's content. I will be wrapped up in train history and the ghost tour all day. I think you'll like where we're staying, despite the name. Their website said the

Hangman's Inn is a historical location. It was originally the courthouse for the whole county, and the pictures showed a garden filled with Roses and Clematis vines." He tries to offer his persnickety wife something to chew on other than his ear.

"Fine. I'll try to overlook the gruesome name. Come on Randy, let's use the restroom before we get back on the road. Read, you go wrangle Rave, she needs to use the facilities here, so we don't have to make any more stops. If there's truly a decent garden at the inn, I'd like to see it before dark."

The brow beaten man collects the family's trash and takes Rogue to look for Rave as he dumps the remains of their lunch in the bin. Rave is on a bench overlooking a stream with her headphones resting like a crown, oblivious to her surroundings. Read has heard his wife hound the girl about being safety conscious while listening to her music, he understands why his daughter is frustrated with her mother. He's frustrated with her too, but what are his options? Divorce? Nope, not for him, not after growing up with divorced parents who shuffled him back and forth using him as a pawn in their mutual hatred. He sighs and taps Rave on the shoulder.

She jolts and rips off her head gear, "Geez, dad! Don't sneak up on me like that!"

"Your mother wants you to use the restroom so we can get back on the road. We aren't stopping again."

She makes an exasperated sound, hooks her headphones around her neck, and stomps off towards the building marked, *Restroom.* Read offers the sweet dog some water and then takes him into the men's room. Random is just coming out of a stall.

"I'll take him after I wash my hands."

"Thanks. See if you can get him to pee one more time, maybe if you walk him by the tree where he already went, he'll go again."

Random dries his hands with a paper towel from the stack on the sink and takes the leash from his father.

Once they're all seated in the car and buckled up, they get back onto Route Thirteen and continue Northwest over the low hills and winding asphalt. Some of the leaves are beginning to turn yellow and a few have fallen across the road. The sun dips behind the trees and the road is darkened with shadows. Read has a feeling of foreboding rippling along his spine, and he brushes it off ignoring his instincts as they desperately try to warn him. What could possibly be wrong with a quaint bed and breakfast in the beautiful foothills of the biggest mountains in the South?

Hoping he won't find out the answer to that question, Read focuses on the road while Rail enjoys the scenery.

A river follows along the road and the woods look like a fairytale painted with the bright colors of fall leaves. They only see a few scattered houses and none of them look occupied. They all seem to have that vacant look a property gets when no one has been there for an extended amount of time.

After what feels like forever to Rave, they finally pass a sign announcing they've arrived in *Hangman's Bluff, The Friendliest Town in the South.* Out of the corner of her eye, she sees a shadow shift behind a tree as they drive by. It looked like a person, but not, he was too tall and too bent. Or maybe he was wearing a strange tall hat? She shakes it off as her imagination but it's difficult to swallow as she continues to watch the woods with a chill in her chest.

Random squirms in his seat next to her and Rogue whines under his breath. She turned off her music when they passed the sign marking the town limits in hopes they were finally going to stop at their destination. But so far there's no evidence of a town, just endless woods.

"How much farther is it?"

"I don't know. The navigation isn't working right. It keeps wanting me to turn around, but it says our turn off is in three miles. Watch for *Hanging Dog Road.*"

"What on Earth is wrong with these people? Why are they so fascinated with hanging things?" Rail complains with the rhetorical question.

"It's probably a joke. You know, since the town is Hangman's Bluff, why not lean into it and mark some other things with equally gruesome names making it funny instead of spooky?"

"Hmpf. Well, the gardens better be as nice as advertised or I'm going to be very disappointed."

"Do we have our own rooms, Dad?" Random asks, hopefully.

"Yes and no. You and Rave have adjoining rooms, and you share a bathroom between you. Mom and I are across the hall, it's not a big place so I don't think there will be more than two or three other families staying there."

Rave asks, "Is there a mall anywhere around here?"

"Sorry. But there's a downtown market center. It says there's an array of small shops all around the town square. There's an art gallery, a book shop, and an antique store."

Not willing to reveal any excitement to her parents, Rave answers with one word, "Cool."

Rail calls out, "There's the turn."

The road narrows as he turns onto a lesser maintained track. They move away from the river and into the woods. As they come up over a rise, the forest begins to thin out and they're surrounded by some green pastures containing horses and cows. A farmhouse and barn dots almost every penned in property.

Finally Read spots an old wooden sign dangling from just one hook, the other having rusted away leaving the sign askew. It says, *Hang Blu In* on the part he can see. He navigates the narrow turn and climbs uphill to the ancient, blue-roofed, Victorian structure perched at the peak. As they pull into the circular drive, in front of the entrance, the house seems to loom over them. It's four stories with lots of windows, dormers, chimneys, and extravagant architectural features which would be charming on any other building. The siding is a faded gray and the shutters are blue matching the high peaked roof. The front door is a deep crimson, it looks like the entrance to hell. A chimney graces each side of the edifice promising a warm fire in multiple rooms, Read hopes their room will be appointed with such a feature.

"Okay everyone, we're here. Let's grab everything and see if we can do this in one trip."

CHAPTER TWO

The family pushes through the heavy red portal loaded with all of their luggage. Read leaves his bags near the front door. The rest of the family dumps their items with his and enters the open front room. It looks like a Victorian parlor from the damask wall coverings to the velvet clad torturously straight-backed furniture. Rave and Randy investigate the room, afraid to sit or touch anything.

The lamps are dressed in dangling crystals and hand painted porcelain shades. Rail has never seen so many doilies in her life, every surface in the room is covered in white crocheted fabric. It feels like a cross between painfully formal and a house of ill repute. Rave likes it. Randy desperately wants to touch an ancient model airplane resting on a shelf in the dark wood apothecary cabinet nestled on the far side of the large room. The ceilings are high, and heavy drapes hang from the top of the crown molding all the way to the hand-stained hardwood floors below on either side of the blurry windows.

Read approaches what appears to be an old banker's counter. It has a variety of cubbies, drawers, and cabinet doors. There's a bell resting on top of the makeshift hotel style desk and he taps it with his finger causing the sound to ring out, startling Rave.

"Hello folks! How can I help y'all?" An average looking man of average height and build asks as he approaches from an arched doorway behind the counter.

"I'm Read Ripley, we have a reservation." The man looks over his glasses at the rest of the family mulling around the front room.

"I see. Yes, here you are, Ripley. Party of four, two rooms one of them adjoining, five nights," he states as he consults a large register sprawled on the desk.

"That's us, and a dog."

"Hmmm, ah yes, and a dog. I see you paid in full online, I'll need your identification, and a credit card for incidentals."

"Are you going to charge something on my card?"

"Not unless you incur any expenses." Rave watches her father hand over his card and driver's license. She studies the man and realizes when he walks away, she can't picture what he looked like. He had muddy brown hair and he was about the same size as her father, but his features escape her. She feels her forehead and ponders if she could be coming down with something.

"All right, Mr. Ripley, just sign here, and here. I have your keys, you're at the top of the stairs, turn right when you get there and both doors on that hallway are yours."

"What time is breakfast? And would you please recommend some place close for dinner?"

The clerk slides Read's cards across the wood countertop and places two keys in front of him. Rave watches intently determined to note every feature of the average looking man.

"Breakfast service begins at seven and ends at ten. As long as you're seated by ten, we'll serve you. The dining room is through that archway." He points to the opening opposite the parlor disguised as a brothel.

"Here's a map with some restaurants, and town isn't far. If you park at the Mercantile, you can walk to any of the places listed. You're all set." He places a printed page in front of Read while he tucks away his cards, pockets the keys, and hands the page to his wife.

"Which way are the gardens on the property?" Rail asks before the man can step away.

He assesses her before answering, "There's a door to the back patio in the dining room, you can access the garden from there. Be careful, there's an angry crow that's been harassing the gardener. Good day."

Rail watches with her mouth open as the man disappears behind the desk, through the doorway and into darkness that seems to swallow him. The oddest feeling comes over her as she struggles to recall what the man looked like or his name. Did he tell them his name?

"Come on gang, grab your bags. Randy, just take your backpack and Rogue, I'll get your bag."

The family climbs the stairs and turns into their reserved hallway, when they reach the first door Read digs the keys out of his pocket. He didn't notice until now that they're ancient keys in sync with the Victorian décor. He pushes one metal key into the keyhole on the door and tries to turn it.

"Of course, it's the wrong key." He checks the door for a number and then the key, finding no marker on either. He swaps the key for the one in his pocket and tries again with success. The room is overly frilly. The twin beds are tall with little step stools to assist with the height.

"Geez dad, it looks like an old lady was trapped in here with a sewing machine. What's with all the ruffles?" Rave queries, never one to keep her opinions to herself.

"It's the style of the place, a few frills aren't going to kill you. Get unpacked and check your bathroom, make sure there's hot water and everything works. We'll get you for dinner in half an hour. Please help your brother." She rolls her eyes, and he ignores it, convinced they're going to have a wonderful family vacation even if he has to force it down the girl's throat.

"I hope our room isn't decorated like that. You know all those ruffles are just full of dust, my allergies will go nuts if I'm stuck sleeping in a dust factory. Why did you choose this place again?" Rail not so passively addresses her spouse.

Read works quickly to get their door opened so she can get it out of her system all at once. Whatever complaints she has about the room can be dealt with swiftly so they can move on to the enjoyable portion of the trip. He breathes a sigh of relief when the door opens upon a *smooth* room. No ruffles or frills of any kind crowd their room and he grins, thinking to himself that she'll have nothing to complain about now. His righteous smile falls as soon as she walks into the room.

"It's freezing in here. Why is it so cold, is there a thermostat? You know I'll be sick by morning if it's going to be this cold." Rail looks around and pulls back the comforter, sheets, and mattress pad checking for bed bugs.

Dropping Rogue's dog bed in the corner, Read wheels their suitcase to the bench beneath the window. Rogue bounces happily into his bed and curls up to watch the people who feed him. Read opens a door to find a generous closet, and another reveals the ensuite bath. It has two sinks in an antique vanity adorned with period appropriate mirrors, and an enormous claw foot tub takes up one corner. Thankfully, the other corner contains a shower and not even Rail could find fault with that.

After they unpack and Rail wipes every surface with sanitizer, they knock on the children's door and the family heads to town for a meal. The highly forgettable clerk was right, the Mercantile isn't far and provides ample parking. The town is mostly dog friendly, and Read wonders if that's why they're the *Friendliest Town.*

Without much effort, they locate an American Bistro with an outdoor patio that allows dogs. The waitress even brings over a water bowl for Rogue and offers him a treat. Random is completely mesmerized by the attention paid to Rogue, he finds it fascinating a restaurant would serve a dog like any customer. The dog doesn't understand why, he's just happy to have the attention, and even though he's easy going, he can be a little needy. It's why they brought him, Read worried he'd be miserable without them.

After the satisfying meal they decide to see a little more of the town. Rave agrees in hopes she can visit the bookshop. Rail wants to ask about the gardens and Read is just happy to walk Rogue. Nobody asks or cares if Randy is okay with a walk, as the youngest his thoughts and wishes are often ignored. Like Rogue, he's easy going and it doesn't bother him.

"I'm going to that shop since I skipped the gardens at the inn, I'm going to spend some money. I'll meet you back at the car in a half hour," Rail announces with a smirk and aims for the Garden Emporium across the way. Rave tries her luck after her mother walks away.

"I'm going to the book shop. I'll meet you at the car." She doesn't allow any inflection to lift the end of her sentence in question, forcing it to be a statement just like her mother's selfish decree. She holds her breath waiting for a reaction from her father.

"Go ahead, just be at the car in thirty minutes."

"Thanks dad." Suddenly overcome with gratitude and forgetting her commitment to teen angst, she leans up on her tiptoes and kisses his cheek, then takes off before he can change his mind.

"I guess it's just us guys. Where do you want to go, Randy?"

"I don't know. I'm just happy to walk with you and Rogue."

"Good man. Let's check out that park. I bet Rogue will find some good smells over there."

Rogue perks up hearing his name, wagging his tail he happily sniffs his way to the park where he can already see some squirrels in need of chasing. Read considers the town, and the people meandering around the little hub of activity, he wonders if any of them are visitors like his family or if they're locals.

As he and Random walk Rogue along the winding path through the park, it follows the edge of a large pond and has a few ducks floating on its surface. Rogue barks at the feathered creatures and they choose to fly to the far end, away from his joyful invitation to play. While Read watches them take flight, he notices a ripple in the water, a rather large disturbance in the otherwise smooth reflection of the sky.

"Did you see that?"

"See what?" Randy searches for something out of the ordinary.

"There's something in the water. It was big."

"What kind of something?" Randy questions focusing on the central feature of the park.

They leave the path and approach the shoreline. Rogue sniffs at the liquid and chances a lick with his long tongue. He laps at the opaque water and splashes one foot into the pond in his excitement. A ripple projects out from his paw across the surface in a dissipating wave.

Read catches another movement from the corner of his eye.

"There!" he points. "Did you see something move?"

"I don't see anything, dad."

They both scan the pond looking for movement. Read spots another ripple near the ducks.

"By the ducks, watch for something to move over there, I just saw it."

"Oh! Yeah, I saw something!"

They remain poised watching for another disturbance on the surface, hoping to catch a glimpse of the large animal causing the movements. When nothing happens for several moments, Randy spots a chipmunk and gets distracted. Rogue is already sniffing the trail of something near the path disappearing into the woods. They let Rogue lead the way and continue on their walk. Without them to witness, a duck is pulled under by a strange blue tentacle, never to be seen again.

CHAPTER THREE

"Come on! Hurry up, I'm hungry."

"I'll be out in a minute, quit bugging me."

When there's a knock on their door Random calls to his sister, "They're here. You're going to miss breakfast!"

"Good! Go away!"

Randy opens the door for his mother.

"Good morning, where's Rave?"

"In the bathroom, she's been in there forever." He points to the locked door across the room with his eyes rolled up.

"All right. She can find us in the dining room when she's finished. Let's go down for breakfast. Did you sleep okay?"

"I guess. I had some weird dreams, and I kept hearing a weird rattling sound. Did you hear it?"

"I'm not sure I know what you mean by a rattling noise. Was it in your room or outside the door?"

"It was in my room, like chains banging into each other. I think it was in the vent over my bed."

"Show your father after breakfast, he can complain to the manager if it's something they need to fix. I'm going to the botanical garden today, are you going with me?"

"Sorry, Mom, I want to check out the trains with Dad."

"It's okay, I figured you'd prefer the trains. Something sure smells good, let's sit here, dad should be right down."

As Rail and Randy take a seat at a large table another pair sits at a small table opposite them. It's an older couple who looks ready to do some damage at the discount market. They nod at Rail and Randy in greeting and Rail smiles at them in return. Read enters the room and joins them just when the waitress arrives with juice and coffee.

She passes out the coffee to the adults and juice for Random. "Can I get you anything else to drink?"

"May I please have some water?" Randy asks politely.

"You sure can. I think the cook is making some pancakes, if you want, she doesn't mind if kids want to watch, you'll get to be an official taste-tester."

"Can I, Mom?" Randy asks, looking at his tougher parent with pleading eyes and his hands pressed together for good measure.

"Sure. Don't go anywhere but the kitchen."

"I promise."

"Come on kiddo, I'll show you where," the waitress, with Tiffany on her nametag offers. Randy hops from his seat and follows her from the room.

"I hope he doesn't have too much sugar being a taste-tester. Should we bring a pancake back for Rogue?"

"No. He seemed like he had a bit of an upset stomach when I walked him this morning. He kept wanting to eat grass."

"Yuck. I'm glad he didn't vomit in our room."

"Me too. I didn't think to bring anything to clean with if he had an accident or any other messes came up. Are you excited to go to the gardens today?"

"I'm so excited. I read online that they have a rare orchid greenhouse. I'm excited to see what they have in there. How about you, excited about your trains?"

"Yes. They have a special tour today that allows us to take a short ride in the refurbished dining car from the original Shooting Star Line, it's a ghost tour. Randy and I will have lunch there. Do you know if Rave is coming with me?"

"She hasn't said, but I'm certain she's not interested in coming with me. Speak of the devil, there she is, our sweet child," Rail adds the last part under her breath with a hint of sarcasm.

"Where's Randy?" Rave questions.

"He went into the kitchen for pancakes," Read answers with a smile.

"There are pancakes?"

"Apparently, why don't you go find him in the kitchen? He went through that archway." Rail points in the direction she last saw Random.

"Okay."

Rave passes through the archway and can hear kitchen sounds at the end of the hall, she follows the sounds and the delicious smell of bacon and maple. When she enters the kitchen, she's surprised to find Random seated at a two-place round table with a plate of chocolate chip pancakes stacked four high. Her mouth waters.

"Hello? I'm Rave, Randy's sister. May I please have some pancakes too?"

The gray haired and slightly hunched woman turns and looks her over, "You sure can. Have a seat with your brother and I'll fix you right up." The elderly woman chooses a plate from a pile of them and starts flipping pancakes onto it. When she has a good tall stack, she places it in front of Rave, then pushes the syrup toward her.

Rave douses the flat cakes with more sugary liquid than necessary and immediately carves out a chunk shoving the forkful into her mouth.

"Mmmm, vis if fo good!" She mangles her compliment through a mouthful.

"What's this?" Randy asks. He plays with the trim along the edge of the table, flipping up the small photos lined there.

"That… is a Deadly-Go-Round," the cook answers cryptically.

"What's a dead round?" Rave asks, curious now, looking at the faded photos along the edge of the table on her side.

"Deadly-Go-Round. It's like a roulette wheel; it spins and then it stops on a photo with the spinner's assignment lined up with that arrow on top. It's an antique. It was here when the owner bought the place, so we don't know much about it beyond what it's called and how it spins."

"Who are these people in the photos?"

"Those are criminals, murderers, serial killers, the worst of the worst. Pretty much anyone you land on will be guaranteed to be the scariest monster you'd never want to meet."

"Why do they spin? What do you mean, your assignment?"

"Legend has it, if you spin the Deadly-Go-Round whoever it stops on becomes your assignment to kill. If you don't kill them, you can't leave town and eventually they'll kill you, you know if you don't kill them first."

Tiffany buts in, "Elvira! Don't scare them with your silly tales. Let them eat in peace. Kids don't listen to her, she's just trying to scare you because she thinks it's funny. Hurry up and finish your pancakes, your parents will have their food in a minute. Do you want anything else, in addition to the pancakes?"

Randy makes a request for bacon, but Rave is mesmerized by the faces along the edge of the table. She touches each one and looks them over, most of them appear to be mug shots taken when they were arrested, but a few look like they're free and living a normal life. She pushes the edge of the table where the photos attach and moves it back and forth testing how it would spin.

"I don't think you should spin it, what if what Elvira said is true? What if you have to kill the person in the photo to leave town?" Random whispers with trepidation.

"Don't be ridiculous. Obviously, that's not possible, she was just trying to scare you, she probably gets her kicks scaring children."

"It worked. I don't like this weird table, it creeps me out."

"Then maybe you shouldn't watch while I spin it." Rave pulls back on the spinning edge and then pushes it forward, so it gets a good spin. There's a rattling sound as it spins, but the mechanism moves smoothly spinning much faster and longer than Rave expected. When it comes to a stop, she spots the arrow shaped like a diamond pointed at the photos and her arrow is lined up with a photo of a red-haired woman. She lifts the photo on its hinge that's attached to the spinning ring for a better look at the image. She realizes the photo can fold all the way up onto the table so she can read the back of it.

"Sarah Jane Robinson, known as the Boston Borgia, 8-11 victims by poisoning. Caught August 12, 1886, sentenced to death, commuted to life in prison."

"This says she killed 8-11 victims. Freeeeeaky," Rave says in the voice of a cartoon ghost.

"You shouldn't have done that, what if Elvira was telling the truth?" Random whispers to Rave trying not to catch the attention of the old woman working at the stove.

But he didn't need to worry about capturing her attention, she already knew what Rave did, and she had a large, evil smile on her face. She waits patiently for Random to make his spin, she knows he will, they always do. No matter how scared they say they are, nobody can resist the call of the Deadly-Go-Round.

"You should try it. I think it's cool. Maybe you'll land on someone interesting too," Rave tries to entice her brother.

"Nope. I don't even want to touch it. I don't like the rattling noise it makes when it spins. Last night while I was trying to sleep, I heard that same sound."

"It couldn't have been this table. Our room is on the other side of the inn. It's okay if you're chicken, you're just a little kid. Lots of little kids are scared of everything. Even a ridiculous story would be scary for most little kids. Come on, are you done? Let's find Mom and Dad."

"I'm not a chicken. I just don't think we should be doing something we were told not to do."

"A chicken says what?"

"What?"

"See, you're chicken. I told you, it's fine if you're not brave enough, you're still a little kid."

"I'm not that much younger than you, and I'm not chicken." Trying to look brave and more grown than he is, Random puts his hand on the spinning edge of the table and pulls it back before pushing it around the same way his sister did. When he lets go it spins fast, the photos lift from the centrifugal force from the speed. As the ring of photos slows, they fall back down and the diamond arrow on Random's side of the table points to a photo.

He looks at the faded old image of a normal, average looking man, wearing a hat and moustache of the time period. Swallowing hard, hoping his killer isn't as scary as the one Rave landed on. He lifts the photo, tipping it up onto the table to read the back.

"H.H. Holmes, known as the Beast of Chicago. 1 confirmed victim, 9 suspected. Apprehended November 17, 1894. Hanged for his crimes May 7, 1896."

Randy sucks in a nervous breath causing Rave to ask, "What does it say?"

"He was suspected of nine murders and hanged. What do you think will happen now?"

"I think if we don't go out to meet Mom and Dad, they're going to come looking for us. Give me your plate, you get our cups, let's take these to the sink."

Randy collects their cups and looks over his shoulder at the odd table one last time before following her to the sink. She rinses their dishes and places them in the sink to be washed in the dishwasher. They dry their hands and before they leave the room, Rave calls out to the chef.

"Thank you for the pancakes."

"Oh, you're quite welcome. It was my pleasure." Rave frowns as the old woman chuckles under her breath. What's funny? She wonders as she directs her little brother to the dining room where their parents are finishing up.

"How were the pancakes?" Read asks with a huge smile knowing both children have an affinity for the overly sweet breakfast treats.

"They were good," Rave answers without elaborating.

"How were yours, buddy?"

"Good." Random can't bring himself to say more when what feels like an ever-tightening strand of barbed wire is wrapped around his middle, making him feel distracted and nervous.

"You feeling alright sweetie?" Rail asks, noticing Randy is much more subdued than usual, especially after having a big dose of sugar.

"Yeah. Can we go, Dad?" Read gulps the last of his coffee and nods.

"Are you coming with us or your mother, Rave?" The girl looks at her parents and chooses to take her chances with her mother. Even though they don't usually get along for more than five minutes at a time, Rave feels bad leaving her mother alone on vacation, guilt is a tool her mother employs often.

"I'll go with Mom." Rail smiles satisfied and pleasantly surprised, somehow Rave seems much calmer than the angry girl from last night.

"Great! Let's get going. I guess we'll meet back here at what? Five o'clock?" Rail confirms.

"Yeah, that should be plenty of time for us to have the ride and be back. All right let's get going." Read guides Randy back to their room to collect Rogue before going to the front parlor where the shuttle to the train museum will pick them up sometime in the next twenty minutes. The entire train experience is dog friendly, and Read is relieved he doesn't require the pet-sitting services offered by the inn.

Rave and Rail leave in their SUV, heading into town to get to the botanical gardens on the other side of the little metropolis. Rave is quiet and thinking about the red-haired Boston Borgia. Rail is lost in her own day-dreams about orchids. If she finds a rare orchid and can get some cuttings, she might be able to win the annual flower show back home.

CHAPTER FOUR

"Dad? Can I ask you something?" Random queries.

"Always. What's up?"

"Well, something happened at breakfast and now I'm worried about it."

"What happened?" Read asks deeply concerned.

"There's this weird table, Elvira says it's a Deadly-Go-Round, and if you spin it you have to kill the killers or you can't leave town, and I didn't want to spin it. But then Rave spun it, and she said I was a chicken if I wouldn't spin it too and I landed on a serial killer, the Beast of Chicago and she landed on the Boston Borgia, and now we have to kill them so we can go home. But they're already dead so I don't think we can kill them. What if we can't leave because we didn't kill them? The table scares me because it makes the same rattling noise I heard in my room. This place is kinda of spooky. Do you think I'm going to get killed if I don't kill the Holmes guy?"

"Whoa! That's a lot of information. Let me ask some questions to clarify. First of all, who's Elvira?"

"She's the cook who gave me pancakes. She was nice but then she laughed about the table and Tiffany told her not to scare us."

"All right, and Tiffany is the waitress, right? What did you call this table?"

"It's a Deadly-Go-Round, it's in the kitchen and it's round with these pictures all along the edge and if you spin it the arrow lands a killer, and you have to kill them, or they'll kill you." Seeing Random visibly afraid, Read is getting angry with this Elvira person. Why would she tell a little boy about all this killer stuff?

"You said it's in the kitchen, right? Will you show me?"

"I don't want to go back in there, Dad, but I'll show you. It's super creepy." Read and Rogue follow Random to the kitchen at the end of the arched hall. Elvira is still working at the stove. There's another hour of breakfast service but with only a few guests it shouldn't be too difficult for her to keep up with orders.

"Get that beast out of my kitchen!" the elderly chef hollers at Read. He looks down and realizes he's walking into a kitchen with a dog.

He hands the leash to Random, "Hey bud, please take Rogue into the hallway and wait there for me, okay?"

"Okay, come on Rogue." The boy leads the dog into the hall and relief floods him as soon as he's able to escape the room with that horrific table.

Read approaches the woman who's sweaty and red faced from standing over a hot stove. She stirs something in a pot, and he can't identify the brown substance.

"I'm terribly sorry for bringing the dog in, I wasn't thinking. I wanted to speak to you about your scary story. It upset my son and now he's terrified he's going to die because of it. I just wanted to let you know and ask you to avoid telling him any more stories. He's quite scared of some table."

"It's not technically a table even though we use it as one but it's much more. It's a Deadly-Go-Round, it's a divination device that connects the spinner's soul with the spirit of the killer on the wheel. It connects them and requires them to kill the assigned killer before they get loose in your world and kill the spinner instead."

"That's crazy, please stop telling my son anything about it. Where is this table?" Read glances around and spots a table with a few plates on it. He moves in for a closer look and reaches out to touch the cards.

"Be careful, if you spin it, you'll need to kill the murderer you land on too." He chuckles at how hard she's selling it. Maybe the inn is trying to get the ghost hunting crowd to stay here. He imagines it would be lucrative with how old and spooky this whole town seems to be.

He pushes a little harder on the edge trying to get a feel for how the thing works. He tries to look at the photos closest to him to see if they're anyone whose name he's heard before and he notices a tension in his stomach, Randy is right this thing is creepy. When he leans down over the table, one of the killers catching his eye, his hand slips against the spinning ring at the top edge where it meets the table. His mistaken brush against the ring sends it spinning and he marvels at how fast it spins when he barely bumped it. The cards with the killers lift again with the force of the movement. When the ring of cards slows, the diamond-shaped arrow in front of Read points to card after card until it comes to rest precisely in the middle of a card.

Read looks at the image on his card and it's a little difficult to see much more than a shape which is most definitely a human. He lifts the card seeking a better view and more information. He realizes he can flip the card onto the table and reads the back with some surprise.

"Ed Gein, also known as The Butcher of Plainfield. 2 confirmed murders, 7 more suspected, and 9 mutilated corpses from the local cemetery. Apprehended November 16, 1957. Sentenced to a maximum-security mental health facility until death July 26, 1984."

Read removes his hands from the table post haste. He's heard of this murderer and recognizes that a couple movies are loosely based on this particular serial killer. The Texas Chainsaw Massacre and Silence of the Lambs are both inspired by the disturbing behavior of this very mentally ill man.

"It won't help to stop touching it now. You've spun, you have to kill him, or you won't be able to leave, and he'll come after you."

"You know you sound crazy when you say that, right?" Read asked the obviously disturbed cook. Her eyes narrow as she evaluates him, her lips pressed together, she seems to determine him lacking.

"You can think I'm crazy, but soon enough you'll find out I'm right. My advice is to strike fast. As soon as you see him, kill him right away so he doesn't have any chance to come after you. You should probably help your kids too, make sure they act quickly, as soon as they spot theirs."

Woof! Woof! Rogue rushes into the room, his leash dragging the ground behind him and barking at the woman, he runs to the table and jumps up putting his front paws against the Deadly-Go-Round. His paws scrape against the table's surface as he continues to bark aggressively and completely out of character for the easy-going K-9.

"I'm sorry dad! He freaked out and took off pulling the leash right out of my hand."

"It's all right, just take him back out." Read moves to help Randy gather Rogue and retrieve his leash. When they get him down off the table, the ring is spinning. Rogue must've knocked it into motion with his angry barks and large paws.

When it comes to a stop, Read and Randy are joined by Rogue to see who it stopped on. Rogue almost looks like he's examining the photo of a man, he then presses his nose beneath the card and flips it up onto the table and looks at Read expectantly.

"This is crazy, did you see that?" he asks Randy.

"I told you it was weird. What does his card say?"

"Theodore Robert Bundy, also known as Ted Bundy. Victims: 20 confirmed, 30 confessed, 36+ suspected. Apprehended August 16, 1975. Executed by electric chair January 24, 1989."

Rogue sneezes. Then he pulls on the leash in Randy's hand taking him from the room. Read isn't sure what to do or say now. He eyes the old woman and takes in a deep breath to fortify himself.

"I'm leaving, we're going on the shuttle to the train museum. Please, just don't talk to Randy about this anymore. Thank you."

"Remember what I said, strike fast. Good luck to you." She turns back to the pot on the stove, and he opens his mouth to admonish her for perpetuating the ridiculous tale but closes it again with a small smacking sound. It just seems pointless to say anything else. He leaves to find his boys. Even though Read is reluctant to leave Rogue behind in the hotel, he decides to stick with the plan.

CONTINUE this story here:

https://a.co/d/063L4RbP

www.ingramcontent.com/pod-product-compliance
Lightning Source LLC
La Vergne TN
LVHW011031110826
845149LV00015B/3374

* 9 7 9 8 9 9 0 9 5 5 6 7 7 *